Snow Children

Masako Yamashita

Groundwood Books · House of Anansi Press
Toronto Berkeley

Copyright © 2012 by Masako Yamashita
Published in Canada and the USA in 2012 by Groundwood Books

Groundwood Books / House of Anansi Press
110 Spadina Avenue, Suite 801, Toronto, Ontario M5V 2K4
or c/o Publishers Group West
1700 Fourth Street, Berkeley, CA 94710

We acknowledge for their financial support of our publishing program the
Canada Book Fund (CBF).

Library and Archives Canada Cataloguing in Publication
Yamashita, Masako
Snow children / Masako Yamashita, author and illustrator.
ISBN 978-1-55498-144-1
I. Title.
PZ7.Y2125Sn 2012   j895.6'36   C2012-900742-0

The illustrations were done in watercolor and Japanese paper collage.
Design by Michael Solomon
Printed and bound in China

For my daughters, Ryoko and Akiko,
for the valuable inspiration they
have given me.

The world is getting warmer. This means
more rain and snow,
violent storms,
heat waves,
droughts,
warmer oceans,
rising sea levels,

melting ice in the
Arctic and Antarctic,

melting glaciers,

less fresh water,

and changes in animals'
environments that they don't
have time to get used to.

But there is still time to slow global
warming if we all agree to work together!

Yuta and Yuna are at the ice festival. It's usually so much fun, but this year all the ice creatures seem sad and droopy.

"*Mmm.* I love this warm weather," says Yuna.
"I love the bright sun."
"I'm hot," says Yuta. "I feel like I might melt."

"I hear there's going to be a meeting about
how hot it's getting," says Yuta. "We should go."

"I want to stay here," says Yuna. "It's a beautiful warm night for looking at the stars. Who needs meetings?"

But sure enough the very next night the sky is
awash with beautiful northern lights. They are
announcing the meeting.

"Come on, Yuna. Let's go and see what's happening," says Yuta.

"Okay," Yuna finally agrees, even though she doesn't really want to.

So off they go, scooting over the snow.

But what's that weak whimpering sound they hear under their feet? Yuta and Yuna dig down as fast as they can. They find a whole family of rabbits.

"Oh dear, oh dear! An avalanche just came out of nowhere and buried us," says Mother Rabbit. "We were so scared."

The rabbit babies cling to Yuta.

"We never used to worry about avalanches around here," says Father Rabbit. "But nowadays it's so warm they seem to happen all the time."

"I hope you'll be okay now," says Yuna. "We'd better get going."

Off they scoot, faster this time, as the rabbits wave good-bye.

When Yuta and Yuna reach the Arctic sea, they see polar bears floating on ice floes. The bears are roaring and groaning.

"What's wrong?" asks Yuta.

"We can't go out on the ice anymore," says a big bear. "We used to hunt for miles, running over the frozen ocean. Now it's so warm the ice keeps breaking, and we can't get to our food."

"I'm hungry!" complains the baby bear.

"I feel so bad I can't help you right now," says Yuna. "Come on, Yuta. Let's rush to the meeting."

Before long they bump into a very large caribou family. The caribou are standing around looking confused.

"Oh no! What's the matter?" asks Yuna.

"Well, we don't know what to do. It's getting too hard to dig through all the snow for the food we need to eat."

Yuta and Yuna look at each other.

"Oh, oh," they seem to say. "What can we do?"

Just then the northern lights swoop down and carry Yuta and Yuna up into the sky. They see all kinds of snow people rushing through the night. That makes them feel better. At least they aren't alone.

When they get to the ice hotel they see
snow people from all around the world
gathered together.

The speaker bangs his mace.
"Welcome, snow people. We've got lots to
think about! But first, let's eat!"

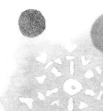

What a feast. There are balls of snow in all different flavors. The snow from the north is crispy. The snow from the foothills of the great mountains is sweet and soft.

"This sweet snow is yummy," says Yuna.

But as soon as the meeting begins, the snow people start to disagree.

"It's too warm."

"It won't last."

"I like my life the way it is. I'm not worried."

"This is a crisis!"

Yuta and Yuna feel shy,
but they think they'd better
say something. So they tell
all about the rabbits, the
polar bears and the caribou.

But everyone still disagrees.
"Colder is better," say some.

"Maybe, but what can we do about the heat?"
say others.
Yuta and Yuna start to feel discouraged.

Suddenly, beautiful shimmering snowflakes begin to fall. As the snow people dance and rejoice they start to feel better.

Yuta and Yuna call out to their friends. "Let's save this beautiful world before it's too late!"

They hear voices saying, "Yes, yes, yes, we must."

The speaker asks, "Have we agreed that we need to find a way to work together?"

Yuta and Yuna finally arrive back home. They tell their friends everything that they've seen and heard.

And sure enough, when their friends hear
about the rabbits, the polar bears and the caribou,
they decide to join Yuta and Yuna.

"The world is getting warmer. Let's try to do something about it. The first step was to get together," say Yuta and Yuna. "Now let's get to work."

What can children do about global warming?

The most important thing we can do to slow global warming is to use less energy. Here are some ideas:

* Walk, bike or take the bus or subway instead of going in a car.
* Play outside or read instead of using computers and video games all day.
* Turn out the lights when you leave a room.
* Turn off the TV when you're not watching it.